Dear Parents:

Congratulations! Your child is taking the first steps on an exciting journey. The destination? Independent reading!

STEP INTO READING® will help your child get there. The program offers five steps to reading success. Each step includes fun stories and colorful art or photographs. In addition to original fiction and books with favorite characters, there are Step into Reading Non-Fiction Readers, Phonics Readers and Boxed Sets, Sticker Readers, and Comic Readers—a complete literacy program with something to interest every child.

Learning to Read, Step by Step!

Ready to Read Preschool–Kindergarten
• big type and easy words • rhyme and rhythm • picture clues
For children who know the alphabet and are eager to begin reading.

Reading with Help Preschool–Grade 1
• basic vocabulary • short sentences • simple stories
For children who recognize familiar words and sound out new words with help.

Reading on Your Own Grades 1–3
• engaging characters • easy-to-follow plots • popular topics
For children who are ready to read on their own.

Reading Paragraphs Grades 2–3
• challenging vocabulary • short paragraphs • exciting stories
For newly independent readers who read simple sentences with confidence.

Ready for Chapters Grades 2–4
• chapters • longer paragraphs • full-color art
For children who want to take the plunge into chapter books but still like colorful pictures.

STEP INTO READING® is designed to give every child a successful reading experience. The grade levels are only guides; children will progress through the steps at their own speed, developing confidence in their reading.

Remember, a lifetime love of reading starts with a single step!

Step into Reading, Random House, and the Random House colophon are registered trademarks of Penguin Random House LLC.

Visit us on the Web!
StepIntoReading.com
rhcbooks.com

Educators and librarians, for a variety of teaching tools, visit us at RHTeachersLibrarians.com

ISBN 978-0-7364-4332-6 (trade) — ISBN 978-0-7364-9031-3 (lib. bdg.)
ISBN 978-0-7364-4333-3 (ebook)

Printed in the United States of America
10 9 8 7 6 5 4 3 2 1

DISNEP

STRANGE WORLD

Adventure Awaits!

adapted by Natasha Bouchard

illustrated by the Disney Storybook Art Team

Random House 🏠 New York

Jaeger Clade is the bravest explorer in Avalonia. He wants to be the first person to explore beyond the mountains.

Jaeger's son is named Searcher.

He is distracted by a plant.

He would rather be a farmer

than an explorer.

Searcher is not like Jaeger.

He is not strong and fearless.

Searcher does not want

to be an explorer.

Jaeger is angry and disappointed.

He leaves Searcher behind

and continues his quest.

Jaeger never returns.

Years later, Searcher farms

glowing plants called Pando.

Pando powers the entire city.

Searcher wants his son

to take over the farm one day.

Searcher's son is named Ethan.
Ethan is growing up and wants
his own life away from the farm.
Searcher embarrasses Ethan
in front of his crush, Diazo.

The leader of Avalonia arrives.
Searcher must join her
on a mission to discover
why the Pando is dying.

Ethan wants to help,
but Searcher tells him
to stay on the farm.
Searcher says goodbye
and leaves for the mission.

To Searcher's surprise,

Ethan sneaks onto the airship.

Ethan's mom, Meridian,

follows in a plane.

Now the whole family

is part of the mission.

Suddenly, flying creatures
attack their ship!
The ship swerves.
Searcher falls off the deck.

Searcher is lost
in a strange world.
It is a beautiful place.

A little round creature steals
Searcher's handkerchief
and runs off.

A hairy creature appears.

It is Jaeger in disguise!

He is still on his journey

after all these years.

Searcher cannot believe

that his father is alive.

In the meantime, Ethan leaves
the ship to find his dad.
He meets the creature that
stole Searcher's handkerchief.
Ethan names it Splat.

Just then, dangerous creatures
called Reapers find Ethan!
Searcher and Jaeger save him.
They try to escape,
but they are trapped.
Meridian rescues the group
just in time.

When they return to the airship,
more Reapers appear!
Jaeger and Searcher aim Pando pods
at the creatures.
The pods shock the Reapers.

After working together,
Jaeger and Searcher begin to
understand each other.
They are different,
but they both want
to be good dads.

Meanwhile, Meridian teaches
Ethan to fly the airship.
Ethan realizes that
he loves to explore.
He wants to discover more
of this strange world.

The crew sees the Reapers
destroying the Pando roots.
The crew smashes Pando pods
into dust and sprays it
at the Reapers.

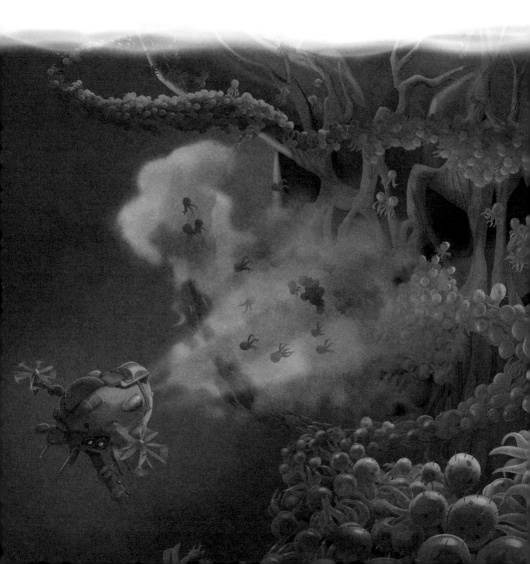

Ethan does not want

to hurt the creatures.

Searcher says it is

a farmer's job to kill pests.

But Ethan does not want

to be a farmer.

Ethan runs away,
and Searcher follows him.
They end up flying
in front of a giant eye!
Avalonia is part
of a living creature.
They realize that the Reapers
are protecting the land.
Pando is destroying it.

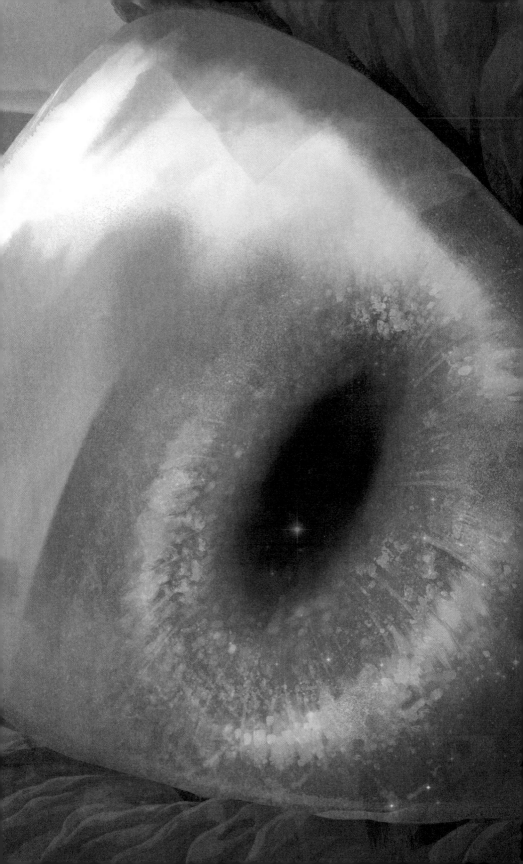

Searcher and Ethan warn the crew
that Pando is dangerous.
The crew does not believe them.
Ethan and Meridian take charge
of the ship.

Searcher and Jaeger dig deep

into the ground so that the Reapers

can get inside the Pando roots.

The Pando is finally destroyed,

but a bolt of energy

knocks Searcher to the ground!

Meridian finds her family
and helps Searcher.
Suddenly, little creatures
begin to heal the land.

Before returning home,
Searcher helps his dad
fulfill his dream.
They see the beautiful ocean
beyond the mountains.

A while later, Ethan introduces
Diazo and his friends to Splat.
Thanks to the Clades,
Avalonia and the strange world
are safe once more.